The King's Robe

Kathy Zuziak

CITI OF BOOKS

CITIOFBOOKS, INC.
3736 Eubank NE Suite A1
Albuquerque, NM 87111-3579
www. citiofbooks. com

Hotline: 1 (877) 389-2759
Fax: 1 (505) 930-7244

Ordering Information:
Quantity sales. Special discounts are available on quantity purchases by corporations, associations, and others. For details, contact the publisher at the address above.

Printed in the United States of America.
ISBN-13:   Paperback   979-8-89391-274-6
                     Hardback   979-8-89391-273-9
                     eBook   979-8-89391-275-3

Library of Congress Control Number: 2024916568

Table of Contents

This book is dedicated to my mother, a beautiful woman of faith.

The King's Robe

By Kathy Zuziak

Introduction

The King's Robe was originally produced as a musical play. It is the story of the Gospel, written in allegorical form, or, if you prefer, a paraphrase. It's not meant to be subtle, or hard to figure out. The King represents Jesus Christ, the Man represents Adam and all mankind, and the wicked servant represents the devil. The narrator of the story is called the Law (Old Testament) up until the time of the resurrection. Then she becomes Grace (New Testament).

Some people seem to try to make the Gospel complicated, but it is simply the story of a rescue, our rescue, yours and mine.

"But I'm fine," you may say, "I don't need rescuing." Oh, but you do! The thing is, it wasn't you that fell into trouble at first. That's why you don't realize the danger. But the trouble was handed down to you from Adam, down to all mankind, and now you're in it, whether you want to be or not.

When Adam chose to obey the devil instead of God, by eating the fruit of the forbidden tree at the devil's bidding, he changed kings and kingdoms. It was a treasonous act. The judgment, or punishment for this act of treachery (sin) was death, which as we shall see, was far reaching.

Spiritual death was instantaneous. Our connection to God is where our life comes from, like a branch is connected to a tree. Spiritual death is simply separation from God, much like a branch dies when cut off from the rest of the tree. Once protected by God and covered with own glory, Adam's evil deed cut him off, and left him vulnerable, naked and afraid. Physical death followed inevitably some years later.

Because man was created in God's very own image, his spirit, the inner man, was designed to live eternally, like God. Even after his flesh and blood body goes back to dust, man will exist forever somewhere. This is where the crime gets more serious. After the earth project, there are only two places where an eternal being can be placed. A sinful creature cannot live in a holy and pure heavenly kingdom, so it must go where its "king," the devil, abides. And we all know that hell is not a desirable location. It is a place of continual torment, and was never meant for man, but for the devil and his thug followers. They don't like it either.

"But it's not my fault!" you may say, "Adam's the one to blame." That may be true, but you are Adam's descendant. He didn't have any children with his wife Eve until after his big mistake, so there is no one who was not affected. Sin was handed down through the blood from generation to generation. Adam's blood, once providing his fleshly body with immortality, was altered to become susceptible to sickness and disease. His flesh was contaminated.

Maybe you didn't do anything wrong or sinful (doubt it), but you're still in trouble because of your bloodline. It's not what you've done, it's who you are. You are in trouble! You are in danger. You need a Savior.

And that's why Jesus made such a big deal of a sacrifice to save you. He gets it! He never wanted to lose you, and still does not want to lose you, even if you don't care a thing about him.

But I'll tell you what, once you get to know him, you will find yourself caring about him too. He's pretty awesome, and the best King there ever was or will be. All praise and honor belongs to You, King Jesus! Forever!

Hmmm, now what's all this about a robe?

"And the son said unto him, Father, I have sinned against heaven, and in thy sight, and am no more worthy to be called thy son. But the father said to his servants, "Bring forth the best robe, and put it on him…"

Luke 15:21 - 22 (KJV)

Chapter One

The Wicked Servant

Once upon a time, there was a King. He was a very, very great and powerful King.

His armies were the finest; thousands upon thousands of the toughest and mightiest of soldiers, perfectly disciplined and ready to defend or attack at his command. But no one threatened him. He was invincible. And his people loved him.

The King lived in a fabulously large palace. It was more beautiful than any other palace ever built. In fact, it was so beautiful that its splendor could be seen from miles away, and sometimes, farmers would stop working in their fields and just gaze at it in awe.

The King's many robes were really something to behold! Spun out of gold and precious stones, they almost glowed when he moved, and everyone wondered at the expert workmanship of such fine clothes. The people were happy that their King looked so grand. "After all, he is the King," they would say, smile, nod, and that was enough.

Now the King had a special servant who was allowed to roam the palace whenever he liked. One day, the King's special servant was wandering down one of the large, golden hallways (I wonder that he did not have anything better to do). As he wandered, a thought came to him, and he turned to the left instead of to the right like he always did. He passed the imposing royal guards, who assumed he must be on official business. Then he headed for the King's private suite of rooms, which was totally off-limits for servants. Stopping at the immense, intricately carved double doors, he gazed with envy at the insignia, which marked the doors as very royal and very private. With a nervous glance over his shoulder, the servant took a big breath. No one was watching (Uh-oh). He silently turned the knob, skillfully hewn from an incredibly large, solid sapphire, and opened the door.

The brightness from the magnificent golden furniture struck his eyes first. Everything was massive and cunningly carved by master craftsmen. On second look, he realized the furniture was not made of gold, but of wood, and each piece appeared to be attached to live trees growing from floor to ceiling, dripping with fruit of every kind. The overall impression was a continuous flow of life. The walls of the room seemed to sparkle as if they were made of diamonds, but as the servant looked more closely, it was little delicate waterfalls flowing down the walls. There were vases of a variety of flowers, that seemed to sing, filling the air with their soft music. The servant thought he heard the splash of some sort of creature and decided there must be a pond or stream running through the room. Was it a room? It was much larger on the inside than it had seemed on the outside. Everywhere he looked there was life! There were even little live creatures with wings, red and blue and yellow and, oh, every color, sitting on the branches of the trees. Some chirped and some preened, and they all seemed completely unafraid and content. But of all these wonderful things, the most noticeable sense was a sweet scent lingering on everything, as if the King himself were present. It was beautiful, no…, more than that. It was miraculous! He had never seen anything like it. And he began to desire it for himself. What would it be like to be the King?

The servant entered the room. He had always wanted to see where the King slept. At least, that is the excuse he gave himself upon intruding into the King's private domain. He looked around, fascinated by the world he had discovered, but there was no bed to be found. Did the King sleep on a chair or on the floor? The servant tiptoed over to an adjoining room. No bed there either. The King must sleep somewhere! But in the search for the King's bed, the servant spied something far more interesting...the King's closet! The closet was filled with glorious, marvelous, splendid clothes, richer than anything he had ever seen in his life! Why, the King didn't even wear all of them! The servant began to drool a bit. (I'm wondering about this guy) "What if I just tried one on?" he thought. Could he be blamed for just trying one on?

Carefully, he selected the most beautiful robe, spun from the blue of heaven itself, and slipped first one arm in, then the other...and that's when something strange began to happen, The servant (I use this term loosely) seemed to tremble. He could feel the power of the authority in the robe. He began to see himself as the King.

Oh, the riches! Oh, the power! The servant's eyes turned glazy, and he laughed, quietly at first, then louder until his whole body shook with evil delight.

"If I were king, I'd show the kingdom who's boss!" declared the servant. "I'd tax the farmers and make them pay. I'd take their sons and make them fight in my armies. I'd take their daughters and make them be my slaves at the palace and in the vineyards and fields. I'd take their fields as well, and their best cattle and their best houses…"

Oh, he went on and on. He couldn't seem to stop!

"I'd have bigger armies to conquer and kill everyone who didn't bow down to me! I'd build big prisons with torture chambers for my enemies. This palace doesn't even have a dungeon," he complained with disgust. He didn't notice that the King had entered the room and was watching his servant's performance quietly. "I'd know how to be a king, all right. I'd be richer than rich! I'd be…" The King could stand it no longer and had to interrupt.

"A terrible king!" The servant whirled around to see the King standing there with his arms folded. "There is more to being a king than having power over everyone. Take off that robe!" he commanded. The servant obeyed and slowly removed the powerful robe.

For now, he thought. The effects of the robe were still throbbing throughout his body.

The King took the robe from the servant. He smoothed the folds of material fondly and then said softly, "A king loves his people. He wants the best for them and wants them to be happy. That is what being a true king is all about. Loving, helping, protecting, sharing the good riches of the kingdom."

He smiled benevolently at the servant. "It is a lot like being a shepherd."

The servant, practically choking on the words, spat, "A shepherd? Bah! Take their sons and daughters and make them slaves! Steal their money for the treasury! Destroy their homes if they won't give in!" He was so upset he had begun to wheeze. Why was the King so weak?

Didn't he understand? The purpose of power was to use it!

The King shook his head sadly. "That is not the heart of a king. If you cannot be a good servant, you will never be a good king." The wicked servant, for so he was revealed to be, backed away, expecting to be immediately cast into irons.

But upon sensing the King's reluctance to punish him, he ventured to speak again.

"I don't believe it! Power, force, and violence are the way to run a kingdom!" He slid his hands over his arms where the robe had been. He could still remember the strength of its authority.

But now the King had had enough. He replied in a strong voice. "No! Your kingdom would crumble after a while. Your way breeds rebellion, destruction, and…death. There is only one way to have an everlasting kingdom."

Then, in a deep, authoritative voice, that some people say sounded like the thundering of many waterfalls, the King proclaimed…

"You shall no longer be my special servant! But that you may learn the ways of a true king, I will allow you to watch what I will do." There was a great flash of lighting and a trumpet blared. The servant cried out in fear and fell to his knees in front of the King.

Chapter Two

The Garden

In the midst of the garden, the wicked servant paced up and down, hands behind his back, biting on his lower lip. "I've got to find a way to get that robe!"

He had not forgotten the feel of it and the power of its authority. It was intoxicating to him, and he was very badly addicted.

"Maybe there's something down here with his precious new Man creature...Uh-oh, someone's coming!" The servant crouched down behind a bush and watched.

A Man, wearing a sparkling blue robe, similar to the one the wicked servant had tried on, walked leisurely in the garden.

He pulled off a piece of fruit from a nearby tree and took a bite. The juice dribbled down his chin and he wiped it off. "Mmmm," he said to himself, "I love this kind! Wonder what I will call it."

The servant panicked. "It's HIM! It's the King!" He cowered lower behind the bush, his face touching the ground. But the Man spotted him anyway.

"Hello, friend. What are you doing in the King's garden?" The servant breathed a huge sigh of relief and stood up. "It's not the King," he thought, "it's just his robe."

The Man spoke again. "I know all the animals here and I don't recognize you."

"Bite your tongue!" The servant growled, "Animal indeed!" Then, thinking it might be in his best interests to appear friendly to the Man, the servant said in a nicer tone, "Let's just say I'm a friend of the family." He brushed the dirt off his plain, servant's garment.

The Man and the servant considered each other, sizing the other one up. The servant couldn't tear his eyes away from the robe, which was clearly royal. He frowned. "Well, isn't this just ducky!" he thought to himself, "The King won't even let me near that robe, and now he's just *given* it to that Man-creature of his! After all I've done for the King, too," He paused. "Er…

What have I done, you ask?" (No one was asking.) "I have graced his palace with my presence! *I* should be the one to wear that fine, beautiful, expensive…powerful robe!" Would the effects of trying on the King's robe *never* wear off?

"Wait a minute! What if…" An idea began to formulate in his evil mind. In a matter of seconds, he had devised the perfect plan. "If I can get the Man to *give* me his robe, *I* will be the one to rule here. It says so in the law." The Man was looking inquiringly at him.

"Ah," cooed the servant, "Here's our little star of the show."

"Is there something I can do for you, friend?" asked the Man.

"Yes, there is, actually. You can let me try on that robe you're wearing." The wicked servant reached out to touch it but the Man backed away.

"Oh, no, I couldn't do that. The King gave it to me."

"I know, I know," lied the servant, "but he gave me one just like it and I seem to have misplaced it. This garden is so drafty, you know." He pretended to shiver.

The Man did not appear to be moved. "Do you think so?" He pulled a different fruit off the tree closest to him.

"The King always keeps it too cool. He's so cheap. Hmmm... What's that you're eating?"

"Fruit from the Tree of Life. Would you like some?" The Man held out the silvery fruit to the servant, who immediately shrank back.

"No!" he almost shrieked, horrified. Then he realized how fearful he must have sounded and changed his tone of voice. "I mean, gosh, no. I eat from this tree here." He pointed to another tree nearby.

"The Tree of the Knowledge of Good and Evil? Really? The King told me not to eat that fruit." The Man continued to eat the fruit from the Tree of Life, clearly not interested.

The wicked servant continued to speak in a deceptively friendly manner.

"No! You don't say! I don't think he really meant that. He never *means* what he says."

The Man replied, "He sounded like he meant it. Said I'd die if I ate it."

"Die? I think that's just a figure of speech. See? I eat it...all the time...and do I look dead?"

The servant skipped happily over to the Tree of the Knowledge of Good and Evil, patted the tree in several places for effect, grabbed one of its fruits, and took a big bite. "See?"

"I don't think so," objected the Man.

The servant decided to step up his game. "Look, rookie, if you want to experience life, REAL life, you gotta taste a little death with it. Spice it up! Wouldn't you like to know pain – just once? Just to know what it feels like?"

"Umm, not really," the Man replied, tossing away the core of the fruit he had finished.

The servant tried again. "Wouldn't you like to know sickness – just to appreciate being healthy? It's so important to know *both* sides of the picture if you want to be wise." The Man looked up suddenly.

"That sounds reasonable. I mean, ...Did you say, wise?... Like the King?"

The servant pressed his advantage. "Now you're talking, Jack! Get to know REAL life! Just look at it." He plucked another fruit from the forbidden tree and showed it to the Man, rolling it around in his hand. "Doesn't it *look* good?" He began to throw it up in the air and do tricks with it.

"Well..." The Man was still a bit hesitant. The servant put on more pressure. It was crucial to his plan that the Man believed him.

Putting his arm around him, the wicked servant walked the Man around a few steps and back to face the tree.

"There's so much out there to get to know! Failure, poverty, hard work… You've gotta take the bitter with the sweet, you know, to really be wise. That's the spice of life, I always say!" He patted the man on the back.

"But the King says..." started the Man. The wicked servant stopped him.

"Who you gonna believe, sonny boy? The one who's holding out on you… or the friend…"He pointed to himself. "… who really cares what happens to you?"

He held out the fruit temptingly, then pulled it back. He moved around slowly in a circle, holding the fruit just out of the Man's reach, then putting it up to his nose so he could smell the rich scent and see the shimmering rainbow of colors. He put his own mouth close to it and licked his lips. "Mmm, it's soooo good! You've never tasted anything like it. It's one of a kind. And only one bite makes you as wise as the King himself!"

The Man reached for the fruit, but the servant pulled it back and held it out of his reach.

"Not so fast, sonny boy. First, you gotta give me the robe. It's not legal unless you give it to me. Besides, you don't want to get juice all over it, heh-heh-heh!"

At the same time as the Man dropped the robe into the servant's hands, the servant dropped the fruit and it rolled away, causing the Man to have to chase after it. "Sorry," the servant laughed, and put on the beautiful robe.

There was a great sound of thunder as the Man took a bite of that desirable fruit.

"Looks like a storm's coming. You'd better run for it," the wicked servant smiled.

Chapter Three

The Wilderness

And so the wicked servant, (or shall we just call him the devil from now on?) tricked the Man-creature, I mean, the Man, into obeying *him* instead of the King.

Perhaps the Man didn't realize that this would be considered high treason against the King. Perhaps he did.

In any case, he had chosen to give his robe of authority and power to his King's enemy and now mankind would have to face the consequences.

Man: Uh…What *are* the consequences?

Law of Sin and Death: (Holding a book, which is the Word

of the King, the Law) The consequences are that you and your descendants actually have to serve under the rule of your new master, the devil, and his perverted 'wannabe' kingdom.

Man: What is that supposed to mean?

Law: In a nutshell? Suffering. Sickness. Poverty. Death.

Man: Death? So...what the King said about me dying was...

Law: Totally true. The devil lied to you.

Man: He LIED?

Law: Big surprise? You were supposed to take dominion and subdue the earth. Genesis 1:28. You should have thrown that lying deceiver out!

Man: Oh… Well, now what?

Law: Physical death is only part of it. The whole world is now under the law of sin and death. Sin *brings* death: sickness, disease, famine, poverty, pain, grief, loneliness, fear, failure. Trouble of every kind is really just some form of death. Did you see anything like that in the King's garden?

Man: No. Does it help to say I'm sorry? What can I do?

Law: Unfortunately, there's nothing you can do. But maybe the King can do something.

Man: He must hate me now. I'm a traitor. I'm... I…

Law: Uh-oh. Here comes the new ruler. Look at this guy!

The devil struggling with the robe, took it off. The sleeves were all twisted, and it appeared to be upside down. There were several rips and wrinkles that had not been there before. Could it be wearing out? After a minute or two of struggle, the devil got the robe back on, but it was inside out. He didn't notice.

"Something doesn't seem quite right here," he complained to his henchmen servants. "Oh, never mind. Do I look taller? I feel taller."

The devil's servants nodded silently, but very emphatically.

"Do I look stronger? I feel stronger." They nodded vigorously again.

"Do I look handsomer, I mean, more handsome?" All nodded but one, who shook his head slightly. The devil spoke to his nearest servant, pointing to the dissenter. "Have him boiled in oil and dismembered immediately!" The servants carried the screaming dissenter out, arms and legs flailing.

"Now to set up shop. Get me a throne!" The devil's servants scurried around, bumping into each other. (They were not the brightest tools in the shed.) "And a mirror… a large one! *I* am king around here, now!" the devil proclaimed, smiling happily. "I just *love* being king! The whole earth is mine. Even *I* didn't realize the depth of the King's stupidity. He is soooo weak! I should have grabbed the robe a long time ago!" He laughed and twirled around, peering behind him as he twirled so he could see the action of the robe. "Delightful! Let's see… who can I intimidate next..." He hummed a little tune as he thought of the possibilities. He rubbed his hands together. "Ah yes, what's that Man creature up to?"

So, to recap our story...the Man made a big mistake. I mean, we're talking giant, humongous, super-duper goof-up of all time! The King had given him authority or dominion over the entire earth. The robe gave him the authority of the King Himself. Now, the devil had the robe, and he wasn't giving it back, although it didn't look good on him. And the devil wasn't a nice guy.

The Man was in terrible trouble! The devil forced him to carry a large bundle on his back, like a huge backpack, filled with problems. It was so heavy that the Man had to walk hunched over, wherever the devil led him, and when he stumbled and fell, the devil would yank on a large chain that was wrapped around the Man's neck.

With the devil's kingdom on earth came sickness, pain, grief, and a whole truckload of trouble. And... adding to all that was the burden of sin and guilt and condemnation that the Man had to carry around, one that he could never shake off. Such a heavy load on his back!

And the devil took great delight in piling on more and more all the time. It was awful!

Man: Can't we stop for a while? I don't feel so well.

Devil: Don't be such a baby! Other people have way bigger problems than you. At least you don't have a *terminal* illness...Come to think of it, you look worse today. (Pokes him). Does this hurt?

Man: Ow!

Devil: That's not a good sign. (Adds another bundle to his backpack.) Here, load this on. I think you just lost your job. Yep! I'll take that last paycheck.

And grabbing the check with glee, the devil skipped away, leaving the man to slump to the ground, totally and completely defeated.

Chapter Four

The King

The King was now in a tricky position. He could not go in and demand his authority back from the devil, because the Man had of his own free will given it up.

The Man had freely chosen to obey the devil's word instead of the King's word, and by that action, he had traded allegiance…and kings. And the King, having given the Man the right to choose, always honored his word. He couldn't just destroy the devil. Why? Because unfortunately, the Man's nature was now too entangled and dependent upon the devil's kingdom. If the King were to destroy the devil, the Man would also be destroyed.

How about starting over? Couldn't he create another man? No. The King couldn't go back and create another man out of the dust of the earth because the dust was now contaminated with the effects of sin (kind of like radiation fallout). Besides, the King wanted to save THIS Man... because he loved him. The King was faced with a very delicate situation.

Seeing all things and knowing all things, the King looked down at his Man and said sadly,

"Look at him. He thinks I have left him to suffer all his troubles alone..., but I have not. I suffer with you, my people. I feel every pain and hear every heart's cry. You are living in a wasteland, a desert, instead of the fruitful garden I planted for you."

And suddenly he was with the Man, walking closely around him, although the Man could not see him.

"Your tears are not forgotten by me, not for one moment! My enemy has turned on you because he cannot get to me. Can you think I do not see it all? But *you* gave your robe to him.

I cannot steal it back. I tell you; Justice is my name, and I cannot go against my own law. But do not lose heart! Hope in me, my people. Trust in your King. Believe that I am faithful and true.

I will never leave you nor forsake you...I have a plan, a plan to take that burden from off your shoulders. Listen to me, my beloved people. I have a plan to get the robe back!

Law: Now the King was a very clever person. His plan was ingenious! He, himself, would come to rescue his people, but he would come in disguise!

Devil: What's this?

Law: Nothing. Go away. You don't get to hear this part.

Devil: Are you sure? Is something going on? Is it about the robe?

Law: Never mind.

Devil: Ok, if you're sure.

Law: I am. Begone! I'm busy explaining things.

Devil: You don't have to be so crabby about it. All right, I'm going.

Law: Now! (Whispering to the reader) Listen up! The King's coming *himself*, disguised as a baby! That's right, a baby! Born to a virgin – Isaiah 7:14, in the city of Bethlehem – Micah 5:2, (getting excited) from the tribe of Judah – Genesis 49:10, a descendant of David – Isaiah 9:7. These clues and more are all there for the people to see, so they will know their King when he comes to save them (overwhelmed with excitement) !!...The Savior! Shhhhhh!

Devil: Did I hear you say a savior is coming?

Law: Go away! Say, isn't that robe looking a little worse for wear?

Devil: (Looking around to his back) Seems all right to me. Maybe a little frayed. It still works, right?

The Law did not answer so the devil shrugged and left.

Law: So! The King comes as a baby – a little Man-creature himself! He grows up, and when the time is right... BOOM! He grabs the robe!... Wait a minute...

(flipping through some pages of the book) It says here that the devil has to personally *give* him the robe. (Scratching her head) Wow! How's he gonna make the devil do that?

The Law cleared her throat and became official sounding.

Law: The King's plan is bold and daring! He will challenge the devil on his own field and with his own rules. May the best king win!

The King wasted no time. He appeared before the devil, not looking very weak now. The devil was slightly confused but on his guard. They walked slowly around each other, in a circle, like sparring partners, keeping a distance. The devil looked for a vulnerable place to strike, in case of an attack by the King, and then decided to attack first.

"So..." he said sarcastically, *You* are the Savior. Did you come for the robe? He gestured to his garment, once beautiful, but now tattered and hanging in shreds.

"I have my own robe" the King said.

The devil lashed out, "The Man gave me his robe fair and square! It's the law!"

"Fair and square?" the King replied, "Hardly. Nevertheless, you are wearing it."

In an accusing manner, the devil said, "You don't belong here."

The King answered, "I belong with my people."

The devil tried a different tactic.

"Why don't we just team up? We could be good together. Tell ya what I'm gonna do. You let me be the main king, and I let you rule – say on Wednesdays? How does that sound?"

The King declared, "I'll tell you what *I'm* going to do."

With those words, they stopped circling. The devil began to tremble. What was the King going to do? His eyes were full of power and there was no weakness there. "Oh, no," the devil thought, "Is this my end?" He really was a coward and greatly afraid of the King. But as he waited for lightning to strike, the King took off his beautiful robe and laid it down carefully.

He was now merely dressed in the garment of a servant, like the Man.

"Wh-What are you doing?" cried the devil, "Without that robe on...I could just k-kill you and take everything!"

The King didn't move.

The devil's eyes opened wide. "What am I waiting for? Guards! Kill him! Crucify him! Crucify him!" His demon servants ran to do his bidding, dragging away the King. There was a sound of the pounding of nails into the wood in the distance, but all the devil could think about was the robe.

"It's mine! It's all mine!" He picked up the shimmering robe. "No more looking over my shoulder, waiting for the ax to fall, so to speak." He was so excited. "I've won! I've won!"

He called to his servants. "Is he dead yet? Is he dead?" One of his servants returned to report.

"He's dead, my lord. Never even put up a fight. Kind of weird. Wasn't that a little too easy?"

"Nonsense!" proclaimed the devil gleefully. "He's dead! And see my new robe? This other one was wearing out anyway. I can't wait to try it on!! He walked happily away, thinking of nothing but the robe and all the havoc he would release on mankind.

Chapter Five

The Great Exchange

Was this the end? Did the King's plan fail? Why did he give up so easily?

The devil was ready to party! He and all his demon cohorts laughed and danced and twitched and cavorted and high-fived each other until they reached a frenzy. Amid the festivities, one of the devil's servants tapped him on the shoulder.

"Ex-excuse me, my lord," he said timidly, "but something seems to have gone awry."

"Nonsense!" replied the devil. "What could possibly go wrong now?"

The servant bowed a few times. "Well, you see, the King…I mean the Man…I mean the King…I mean he's…he's alive again and he's…"

Just at that moment, a hush fell over the party, for the King himself walked into the group. It parted for him immediately, like the Red Sea. He was carrying a familiar-looking backpack with one finger.

"I've come for the robe devil. You can have *this* back." He threw the backpack on the ground in front of his adversary.

The devil, shocked and afraid stuttered, "B-b-but you…, you're dead! You're in my domain! The law says…"

The King interrupted him. "The law…states that the payment of *sin* is death."

The devil didn't get it.

"So?" he shrugged, "You died. And here you are. Get back in your chains." He turned away, dismissing his prisoner with a flick of his hand.

The King took command of the atmosphere. When he spoke, the silence from the demons was like a black hole. His words carried the full weight of the authority of the law.

"He who sins must die. There was no sin in me, devil, and therefore no payment was required." The devil spun around to stare at the King.

"Wh-What did you say?!"

The King was firm. "You have killed an innocent man. *You* have broken the law and by your own rules, my law-crusading servant, *you* must forfeit the robe. Oh yes, and while you were preoccupied with getting revenge on me, I took the opportunity to take the Man's sin on myself, somewhat like…putting on a robe, shall we say?" (The King chuckled to himself.)

"According to the law, by my sacrificial death, all of Man's sin has been permanently paid for and the Man is free."

The devil, thinking hard, wracked his brain for a loophole.

"But…but…," he stalled, "That can't be right! Er…uh… Just give me a minute."

All his servants looked back and forth, first at him, then the King, then at him, then the King.

 Seeing his servants losing faith in his leadership, the devil cried, "No! No! There must be some mistake! Let me see the book."

One of his servants handed him the book of the law. The devil leafed through its pages, and then he stopped, and traced down one page with his finger, looking slowly up.

"Hmmm, you may be right, heh-heh…but let's not be too hasty." He began to back away from the King.

The King commanded sternly, "Give me the robe, devil, or lose *your* life now – what's left of it!"

The devil, arguing, preparing to give a line of defense, began, "But you can't …" Then he looked into the King's eyes, saw no mercy, and slowly took off the robe. His eyes hopefully and desperately searched the King's face for any sign of weakness, which he could have sworn was always there before, but there was none now. His hands trembled in fear as he gave the robe to his Master.

The King folded his robe lovingly, then spoke prophetically and with authority to his wicked servant, who had begun to shake with dread.

"Your time is short!"

The devil knelt and began to hug the legs of the King. "You know you need me, Your Highness. I'll do anything you say…I'll shine your shoes…remember you are merciful…"

The devil's servants began to point at him and laugh. And the King, much to the astonishment of the devil, did not fall for his false groveling. Instead, he slapped a collar around the devil's neck, attached a long chain leash, the same one the devil had used on the Man, and paraded him around the room like the dog he was. When the devil tried to whine or speak, the King jerked his chain and choked the words out of him until finally the devil just gave up and stopped talking, totally shamed and defeated.

The devil's servants giggled, laughed, and chortled until their sides ached and then the King turned his face to them. He was not smiling. They shrieked and screamed for mercy, cowering and trembling together, each trying to avoid the eyes of the King. His voice boomed out all across the gates of hell.

"ALL authority is given to me in heaven and earth, over every principality and power and might and dominion!" He showed the servants the robe. "Have I made myself quite clear?"

The devil's servants nodded up and down very vigorously.

"There is only one King around here." At these words, he forced the devil down with his face on the ground. He placed his foot firmly on his neck.

The servants all shrank back, gasping in alarm. "His name is JESUS!"

The next moment the King had disappeared. The devil's servants echoed the name Jesus softly, in awe.

"Shut up!" shouted the devil angrily, picking himself up and dusting himself off. "Cowards!"

He ripped his dog collar off, struggled for a moment to remove the chain, then tossed it to the side, rubbing his neck. He began to pace.

"Maybe the people won't notice I don't actually *have* the robe anymore. They're slow. They don't know the scriptures. I don't have to leave. The King didn't *say* I had to leave...

Epilogue

The Robe

So the best king won and the devil was defeated at his own game! The robe was back with the King where it truly belonged.

Back at the castle, the restoration of the King's robe was honored with a grand procession, led by the children waving long, colorful ribbons and palm branches. Young men and women carried in the royal robe with banners flying. The King's royal guards stood on either side of the highway and all the people cheered. Triumphant music played and flowers were strewn everywhere. The birds were singing. It was a time to celebrate, and they did. Finally, the procession drew near to the throne.

On the King's left was his royal Herald. On the King's right was the Man he had saved.

The Man was looking nervously around like he felt out of place. After all, he reasoned, he had been a traitor. He was guilty. The condemnation of his conscience was overpowering.

There was a short trumpet fanfare and then the King's Herald, standing straight and tall, unrolled an official scroll. He proceeded to read it to the people in a loud and official sounding voice.

> Herald: Hear ye! Hear ye! Wherefore, as sin came into the world through one Man, and death as the result of sin, so death spread to all men, no one being able to stop it or to escape its power, because all men have sinned. [1] Wherefore, as one Man's trespass, one Man's false step and falling away led to condemnation for all men…[2]

The Man lowered his eyes to the ground. He was so ashamed. His mistake had led to the failure of all mankind, and the ruin of the King's entire project! He felt like less than a worm.

The Herald continued…

> Herald: …so one Man's act of righteousness led to acquittal and right standing with God and life for all men.[2] Let all mankind rejoice in the victory of their Savior, the King who became a servant so that his people might become kings. All praise to the King of kings and Lord of lords!"

The Man lifted his eyes. What had the Herald said?

The people cheered and cheered for a long time. Then the King's Herald spoke again.

Herald: May the God of our Lord Jesus Christ, the Father of glory grant you a spirit of wisdom and revelation [of insights and mysteries and secrets] in the [deep and intimate] knowledge of Him, by having the eyes of your heart flooded with light so that you can know and understand the hope to which He has called you, and how rich is His glorious inheritance in the saints (His set-apart ones), and [so that you can know and understand)] what is the immeasurable and unlimited and surpassing greatness of His power in and for us who believe, as demonstrated in the working of His mighty strength, which He exerted in Christ when He raised Him from the dead and seated Him at His [own] right hand in the heavenly [places], far above all rule and authority and power and dominion and every name that is named, [above every title that can be conferred], not only in this age and in this world, but also in the age and the world which are to come. [3]

The people again cheered and waved their handkerchiefs, banners, ribbons, and palm branches for a long time.

Then, the King stood and did something amazing. Right there, in front of all those witnesses, he took the robe that had just been returned rightfully to him and placed it on the shoulders of the Man standing next to him. And then he smiled and said to the Man,

King: All power has been given unto me in heaven and in earth.. Go ye, therefore…[4] Behold! I have given *you* authority and power to trample upon serpents and scorpions and [physical and mental strength and ability] over all the power that the enemy [possesses]; and nothing shall in any way harm you. ⁵ When he sees the robe... he will see me. Remember, believe my Word and you will live!

The crowd was silent, waiting to see what the Man would do.

The Man, overcome with amazement, turned to the King. He knelt before Him on one knee and kissed His hand reverently. Then he stood and turned to the crowd. He was no longer ashamed. His guilt had been forgiven and he had been completely restored.

Man: Did you hear that? I've been given a second chance! Mankind has been given a second chance! This is amazing! Marvelous! It's…it's a miracle!

The Man hugged and hugged the King, tears flowing freely from his opened eyes. He was crying, the King was crying, everyone was crying! Then, suddenly realizing he was blocking the King from view, the Man blushed and stepped back, allowing the King to take center stage. The crowd applauded and cheered.

When the applause had died down, the Man said to the King in front of everyone,

Man: Thank you! Thank you, Jesus! You truly are my Savior, my Good Shepherd, my only King! You rescued me from the kingdom of darkness and brought me back into the Kingdom of Light. You alone are worthy of all honor and glory! I won't let you down this time. I'll always believe your Word. I'll serve you forever!

There was no blushing now. He knelt again, in reverence, but this time the King took his hand and raised him up. He looked into his Man's eyes and said in a voice filled with lovingkindness, but loud enough so that everyone could hear and bear witness,

> King: You are no longer a servant, but a son. You shall reign for all eternity alongside me.

He then sat and made room on the throne next to Him. The Man sat down, and the King smiled his biggest smile. The Man smiled too.

> Grace (no longer Law): Well, isn't that amazing! The King turned right around and gave the robe back to the Man. And the Man is now in a *better* position than he was before he fell. That's the kind of King we serve! Now I ask you ladies and gentlemen, children of Adam, believers young and old, what will you do with the robe He has given YOU? The robe that cost him everything, is free to you and me because of his great love for us, his people. Will you accept it? Will you disregard it? Will you give it away? Or will you wear it?

What will you do with the King's robe?

I delight greatly in the Lord; my soul rejoices in my God, for He has clothed me with garments of salvation, and arrayed me in a robe of His righteousness, as a bridegroom adorns his head like a priest and as a bride adorns herself with her jewels."

Isaiah 61:10 (NIV)

Bible References

1. Amplified Bible
    Romans 5:12

2. Amplified Bible
    Romans 5:18

3. Amplified Bible
    Ephesians 1: 17-21

4. King James Version
    Matthew 28: 18-19

5. Amplified Bible
    Luke 10:19

9 798889 391246